THE PERSONAL TRAINER

AN EROTIC ADVENTURE

VICTORIA RUSH

VOLUME 11

JADE'S EROTIC ADVENTURES - BOOK 11

COPYRIGHT

The Personal Trainer © 2018 Victoria Rush

Cover Design © 2018 PhotoMaras

All Rights Reserved

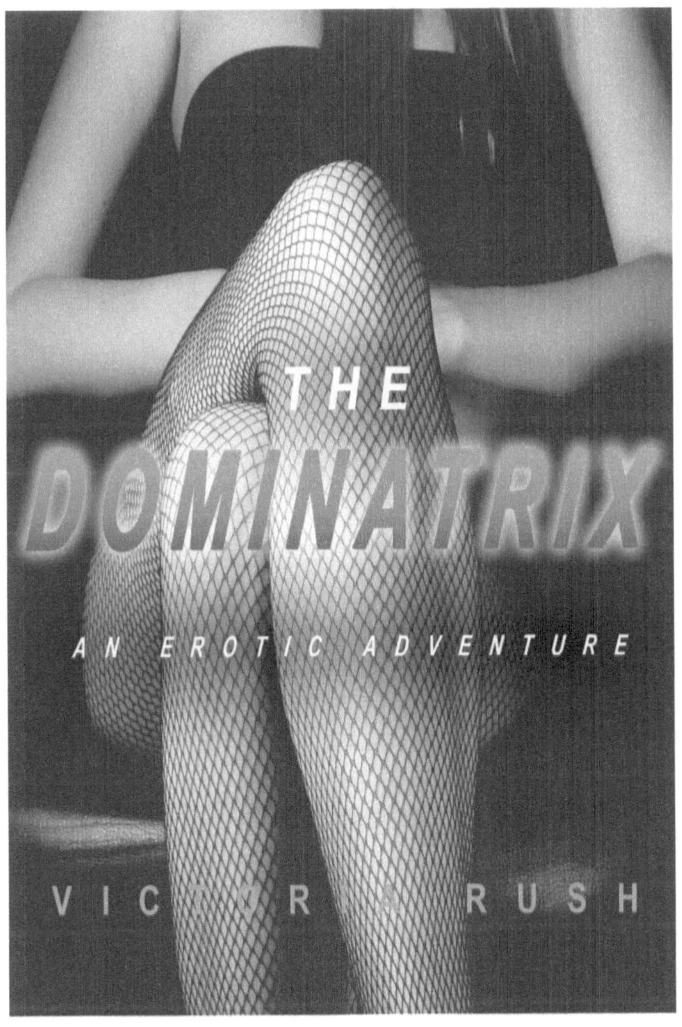

Sometimes it takes a little kink to break out of your usual routine...

Everyone's an exhibitionist in disguise...

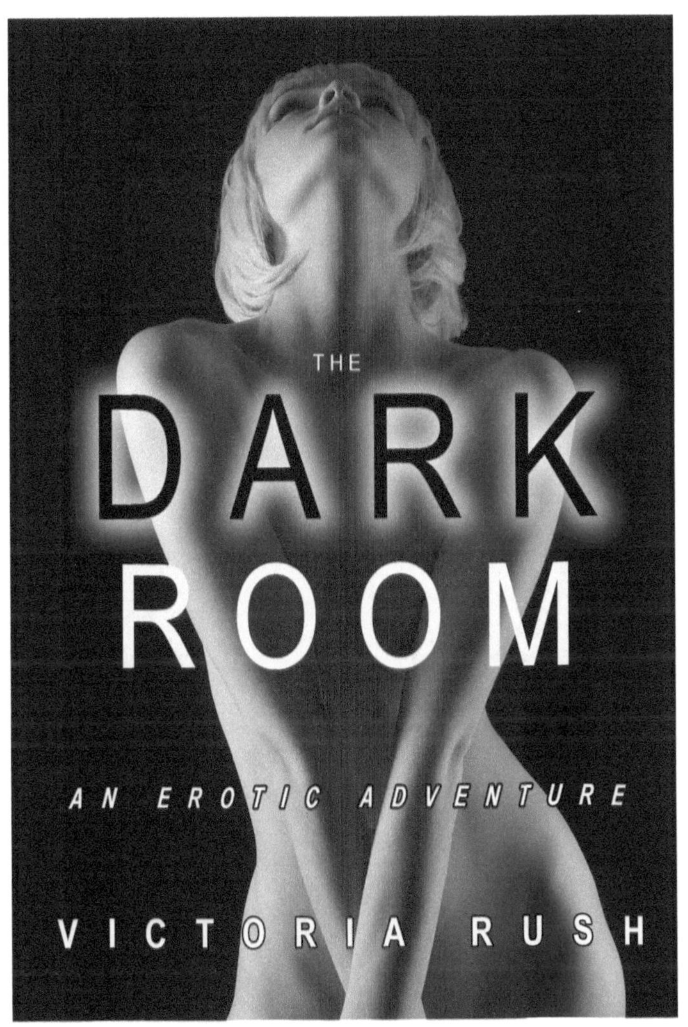

Everything's sexier in the dark...

Mula Bandha is for lovers...

Books 6 - 10 in the bestselling series - now 60% off.

For the uninhibited...

1

PUMPED UP

Over the past few months I'd noticed some unsettling changes in my body appearance. It was nothing drastic—just little things that had been creeping up on me. A slight loosening of the tone on the underside of my arms, softening of my stomach muscles, and tightening of my jeans. I still felt I was in better shape than most women my age, with firm breasts, a tight ass, and shapely legs. But my three-times-a-week yoga sessions focused mostly on stretching and relaxation. It was time to get serious about reconditioning my aging body.

One Saturday morning, I went down to my local health club to talk about my fitness goals. When I stepped through the front door, I was surprised with the level of intensity permeating the gym. Near the front window, a group of scantily clad trainers huffed away on a long bank of tread-mills and elliptical machines. On the side wall, a collection of young women in tight leotards stretched quietly on a padded mat. Near the back of the facility, burly guys in tank tops and loose sweats grunted noisily as they lifted weights.

Virtually everybody was in excellent shape, and as they

moved through their paces, their sinewy muscles rippled under their dewy skin. Feeling a bit intimidated, I was just about to turn around and head out for a coffee to contemplate what I'd gotten myself into, when a cheerful woman's voice addressed me from behind.

"Can I help you with something?" she said.

I turned around and saw a young staff member in tight leotards.

"I was just—looking around," I said. "I'm not sure I'm ready to get started with a weight-training program."

"We've got a lot more than just weights at our club," the girl said. "There's a full complement of cardio devices, Pilates machines, and an aerobics studio if you want something different. Were you looking for a self-paced program, or something with instructional support?"

"I'm kind of new to this sort of thing," I said. "So far, I've mostly just participated in yoga classes..."

"We have those too, if that's what you're most comfortable with. Perhaps you'd like to start with an introductory session with a personal trainer who can assess your fitness goals and design a custom workout program for your individual needs?"

"I suppose that makes the most sense. What are your fees?"

"A complimentary personal training session is included with a three-month trial membership. The basic monthly fee is forty-nine dollars per month, and you can cancel anytime. Additional training sessions are available at negotiated rates, depending on your trainer."

"That seems pretty reasonable," I said. "When are your trainers available?"

"Normally, we need at least forty-eight hours advance

notice for scheduling, but we happen to have one available right now if you'd like to get started today."

I glanced around the gym at all the buff bodies and nodded.

"I think I've stalled long enough already," I said, removing my wallet from my purse. "Let's get the ball rolling."

After I signed the personal waiver and provided my credit card details, the receptionist gave me a combination lock and told me to store my personal effects in the women's locker room. I changed into my yoga tights and when I returned to the reception area, someone else was standing behind the desk. An attractive, athletic woman about my age was scribbling something on a clipboard and looked up.

"You must be Jade," she said, lowering her clipboard.

When she revealed what she was wearing, I gasped. She had on a one-piece black leotard with a large opening in the front of her chest, revealing the muscular cleavage between her large breasts supported by a crisscrossed elastic strap wrapping around her neck. Her breasts were perfectly round and firm, flexing gently as she moved her arms. It was obvious that she wasn't wearing a bra, with her spandex outfit cradling her bosom in a sensuous X-shaped pattern, with the faint protrusion of her bare nipples pressing against the stretchy fabric. Not that she needed one. I was quite sure that her breasts would have sat just as firm and high on her chest without any support whatsoever. Her bare arms and shoulders rippled as she held the clipboard in front of her, and I ran my eyes shamelessly over her body, taking in her exquisite form.

If this is what a little weight-training will do for my body, I thought, *count me in.*

"Um, yes," I stammered, returning my gaze to eye level.

Even her *face* looked sculpted, with sharply-defined cheek-bones, an angular jaw, and full, sensuous lips.

"I'm Kate," she said, extending her hand. "I'll be your personal trainer today."

I clasped her hand and Kate squeezed mine firmly as she smiled at me.

"Why don't we take a few minutes to clarify your fitness goals before we get started?"

She pointed to a tall round table with high stools in the corner behind the reception desk.

"Let's have a seat and get to know each other first."

When she emerged from behind the reception desk and began walking toward the table, my eyes almost bugged out of their sockets. Kate's ass and legs were even more firm and shapely than her arms and tits. Her tight leotard hugged every curve of her round, athletic butt, and her calf muscles flexed sensuously as she walked. When we both took our seats at the table, I exhaled audibly, trying to control my excitement.

"So then," she said, looking at me with her pretty hazel eyes. "What were you hoping to achieve from your training program?"

I had a hard time concentrating with her sharply defined cleavage staring me in the face.

"Just improve my tone, I suppose. Basically, I'd like to look like you. I'm guessing you're pretty close to my same age, but I don't look anything like—*that*."

Kate smiled as she quickly ran her gaze over my arms and chest.

"You've got some good raw material to work with. May I ask your age?"

"Thirty-five," I said.

"You're in great shape for someone—" Kate hesitated, as

she scribbled some notes on my chart. "...our age."

I smiled, feeling more comfortable knowing I'd have a contemporary guiding me through my paces.

"Did you want to focus on any parts in particular?" Kate asked. "Because from my vantage point, everything looks to be pretty nicely balanced."

"It might be balanced, but I'm not honed like you. I'd just like to tighten everything up a little. Reduce my body fat, add a bit more shape to my arms and legs, maybe firm up my ass a little."

"I can work with that," Kate said. "How much time can you afford to invest?"

I chuckled at Kate's implication that this was going to be a long haul.

"Do you think it's going to take that long?"

"I meant per week—per session."

"Oh. I dunno. Will an hour per session, three times a week get me there?"

"It's a good start. As long as you keep at it. I'm sure you've heard the expression *use it or lose it*. Once you begin to make some gains, you can lose them just as quickly if you stop. Personal health and fitness is a journey, not a destination."

I peered up at Kate and smiled.

"That's what I've got *you* for, right? To keep me honest and straight."

"I don't know about the *straight* part, but I might be able to guide you in the right direction."

I paused for a moment, trying to glean Kate's meaning. Was she trying to tell me that she was attracted to women also? Suddenly, my pussy began tingling in excitement.

"It's a deal," I said. "Let's do this."

"Alright then. Let's get started with a short warm up. It's always best to start with some gentle stretching to elongate your muscles and get the blood circulating before you do anything too strenuous. I'm going to suggest you do ten minutes of stretching, followed by a half an hour of lifting, then twenty minutes of cardio as a start."

"Yes ma'am," I said, beginning to feel my blood rushing to other parts of my body already. "Your wish is my command. For the next sixty minutes at least, I'm all yours."

Kate led me to the stretching mat then stood beside me facing the bank of mirrors.

"First, let's loosen up your shoulders with some gentle windmills."

As she began swinging her arms in circles over her shoulders, I watched her tits shaking on her chest while her pectoralis and deltoid muscles flexed. As I mimicked her motion, I pretended to watch myself in the mirror, but the whole time I was fixated on her cleavage jiggling in the center of her chest. As I swung my arms with increasing frenzy, I fantasized about burying my face in her glistening valley.

"Now the other way," Kate said, swinging her arms in the other direction.

After another minute or so, she stopped and turned her body away from the mirrors.

"Now let's loosen up your lower body. Spread your legs about four feet apart then bend at the waist and try to place your palms on the floor between your legs."

Kate lowered her torso in a perfect V-shape and rested her forearms on the mat in front of her. I tried to match her pose, but I could barely get my fingertips to touch the floor.

"Don't worry if you can't get all the way down," she said, noticing my struggle to bend myself as far as she had. "Grip your ankles and gently pull yourself down toward the mat one inch at a time, pausing every fifteen seconds to let your muscles relax. Look between your legs in the mirror to find a setpoint to push yourself a little further."

When I looked between my legs, the only setpoint I could focus on was Kate's exquisite upturned ass staring me in my face. I glanced at the junction of her thighs near the bottom of her ass and detected a slight darkening in the fabric.

Was that sweat, or was she getting as turned on as I was watching her in the mirror?

"Yes," I said, feeling my own juices beginning to accumulate in my pussy. "I can feel things loosening up. My muscles are already relaxing."

"Good," Kate said. "When you get your palms flat on the floor, begin to wiggle your feet closer together, pausing and relaxing every fifteen seconds. You should begin to feel the pressure moving from the inside to the back of your thighs."

"I feel it in—*both* places," I said. But what I really meant to say was that my pussy was burning for an entirely different reason.

Kate led me through another ten minutes of stretching on the mat, with each pose giving me another opportunity to gawk at her magnificent figure. By the time we'd finished the split-knee hip stretch, I didn't want to get up off the mat while I fantasized about comingling our bodies in a more direct manner. Plus I was forming a large wet spot in the crotch of my tights that I was afraid would show if I stood up.

"Okay," she said, suddenly getting up. "I think we've got you plenty warmed up. Let's see if we can start working on that muscle tone you talked about."

She led me to the bench press station where a bar with two forty-five-pound plates rested on the rod. She lay down and lifted the bar off the rests and demonstrated five effortless reps.

"This will help tighten up your chest muscles and provide better support for your breasts," she said as she pumped the bar up and down. "Just remember to lower and raise the bar slowly, always keeping the weights under control. I'll watch you from behind to guide you."

She got up from the bench and motioned for me to lie down. Then she removed the two big plates on opposite ends of the bar and returned them to the stack.

"No weights?" I said, looking up at her inquisitively. "I know you're a lot stronger than me, but I didn't think I was *this* pathetic—"

"The bar alone weighs forty-five pounds," Kate said. "This is typically one of the weaker exercises for women. Let's start low and work our way up. We don't want you hurting yourself on the first day."

I lifted the bar off the rests, surprised at how heavy it felt. As I slowly lowered and raised the bar, Kate stood behind me at the head of the bench, leaning over with her palms just under the bar to catch it if I faltered. Every now and then, she glanced further down my body toward the wet patch between my legs.

"You're doing great, Jade," she said.

But all I could concentrate on was her firm breasts hanging over my head, mere inches away from my face. From this posterior angle, I could appreciate the full weight and shape of her bosom, and my mouth watered whenever she leaned closer, while I fantasized about sucking her protruding nipples. After the sixth rep, I began to grunt, struggling to lift the bar.

"Two more, Jade," Kate said. "Feel the burn. That's the

good kind of pain. It means your muscles are growing stronger."

My pecs weren't the only part of me that was burning watching Kate's tight body hover over me. My sex drive was also growing stronger by the minute.

"Uhnnn!" I grunted, trying to pump out the last rep.

"Good girl. Whenever you can break through your limits, that's when you know you're making gains."

I looked up at Kate, breathing heavily.

"You're not going to make me look like Arnold Schwarzenegger, are you?"

"Don't worry," Kate laughed. "We're just going to push it far enough to improve your muscle tone a little. When you start to see your body fat diminish and your muscles become more prominent, we'll know when to back off."

"I hope so," I said, sitting up on the bench and resting my hands on my thighs, still huffing. "What's next?"

"Let's do something for your butt and thighs now. This one's a little tougher, but it does wonders for your derriere."

Kate walked me over to a vertical weight station where another bar with two large plates on each side rested about shoulder height on the support bars extending from the rack.

"This is the squat station," she said. "This one's a bit more strenuous, so it's super-important you do it slowly and with proper form. Let me show you first."

Kate bent her knees and dipped her head under the bar then lifted herself up with the bar resting on the back of her shoulders.

"Jesus," I said, watching the bar flex from the heavy plates. "Do you ever lower the weight, or do you just lift whatever the guys leave on the bar?"

Kate smiled as she looked at me in the mirror.

"I've been doing this for a while, and this is one of my stronger exercises. But believe me, I still feel it."

Kate proceeded to lower her body with a straight back until her legs were at a ninety-degree angle, then she slowly lifted herself back up to a standing position. As she lowered and raised herself in repeated repetitions, she talked to me as if it were a walk in the park. All the while, I stared at her bubble butt as it stretched and flexed from the strain of the weights.

"Remember to breathe in at the top of the movement, then exhale slowly as you raise yourself back up. Try to keep your back straight and don't go lower than ninety-degrees, so as not to strain your knees too much."

After four or five repetitions, Kate placed the bar back on the supports then stepped back and removed the plates, adding a twenty-five-pound weight on each end.

"That doesn't look like much," I said, disappointed in her lack of confidence in me. "I used to run track at school. I think I can do more than that."

"You probably can," she said. "But let's focus on your form to begin with and work our way up to your max. Remember, you said your goal is to tighten your tone, not add strength or bulk. We'll leave the heavy lifting to the guys."

Kate moved a bench into the center of the station and instructed me to straddle it with my legs.

"This will help give you a little support and let you know how far to go down. Let's do a couple of sets of eight reps to start, trying to touch but not rest your hips on the bench on the way down."

As I spread my legs and straddled the bench, I looked in the mirror, seeing the expanding wet spot in my tights.

"Sorry," I said, glancing between my legs. "I guess all this pumping and burning is getting more than just my muscles worked up."

"Not to worry," Kate smiled. "It does the same thing for me. That's another side benefit to strenuous exercise. It also boosts your sex drive."

I placed my head under the bar as Kate had, and when I lifted the bar off the supports, I immediately regretted asking her to add more weight. I hobbled backwards and slowly began to lower myself to the bench.

"Argh," I groaned, as I flexed my knees and tensed my thighs to support the weight. "You're right. That is pretty heavy. Do I have to go all the way down?"

"Go as far as you feel comfortable," Kate said. "Ease into it at first, lowering yourself more with each rep. You just need to get used to the movement. It won't take long for you to improve your form."

As I moved through each repetition, I watched myself in the mirror. The top of my thighs were burning, but I wanted to show Kate that I wasn't a quitter. When my ass touched the bench on my fourth rep, I was tempted to sit down and rest, but I forced my legs to push myself back up.

"That's it, Jade," Kate said. "That's a good rep. See if you can do four more, touching but not resting on the way down."

Each time my ass touched the bench, I could feel my pussy spreading apart. By the seventh rep, my thighs weren't the only part of me tingling from the heavy exertion.

"One more, Jade," Kate said. "Feel the burn."

"Oh, I'm feeling it alright," I panted.

"Try to push through your limits," she said. "That's what ultimately will help you reach your goals."

"You're pushing me to places I haven't been in quite a

while, Kate," I said, exhaling deeply as I finished the eighth rep.

"Okay, now take a thirty-second rest, then we'll do one more set."

"Are you kidding me?" I protested. "This is my first work-out! Didn't you say I'm supposed to *ease* into this?"

"No pain, no gain, girl," Kate said. "I'm trying to instill a good work ethic so that when I'm not around to push you, you'll remember to push yourself."

I looked up at Kate, realizing how dependent I'd already become on her guidance and supervision.

"How much pain am I going to be feeling tomorrow?" I said, massaging my throbbing thighs.

"You'll probably feel a few aches tomorrow morning. But remember, that just means your muscles are rebuilding and growing stronger. This is the first step to improving your shape, tone, and firmness. You'll thank me later."

She glanced back at the bar resting on the rack.

"Now, one more set."

"Right," I groaned.

I stepped back under the bar and lifted it off the supports then lowered myself toward the bench. I was glad Kate had placed it there to catch me, since my thighs were definitely nearing the point of exhaustion. But I was also glad she'd put it there for another reason. Each time I dipped down and touched the bench between my thighs, I felt a charge run through my body as I rubbed my clit softly against the padded surface. By the time I finished my last rep, a small puddle had formed in the middle of the seat.

"Good job," Kate said. "Don't you feel like you're pushing through your limits already?"

"Definitely getting *close*," I panted, feeling my pussy tingling between my legs.

"Just one more exercise for today," Kate said. "Time to work on your core muscles. This next one is one of my favorites. Not only will it strengthen your midsection, it gives you great definition in your stomach."

Kate led me over to a strange contraption that looked like a cross between an airplane cockpit and a torture rack.

"This is the ab crunch machine," she said, positioning herself in the seat then reaching over her shoulders to grab the support handles.

"Try to pull your upper body down with your arms and lift your lower body up with your legs at the same time, so you work both parts of your abs. If you do it right, you should feel a gentle burning feeling in your stomach muscles."

Kate demonstrated eight perfect abdominal crunches, then she hopped off the machine and motioned for me to get on it. There was a hump in the pad directly in front of my crotch, and as I sat down on the seat, the pad rubbed against my still-tingling clit.

"Focus on pulling your chest down to your hips, curving your spine forward, instead of bending at the hips," she said. "I'm going to stand behind you so I can make sure you're keeping your back in the proper position."

Kate stepped behind the machine, then placed her hand between the two separated pads and touched my lower back.

"Try to keep your back pressed against my fingers as you pull down. Now, lift the weight slowly as far as you can go down."

I tensed my abdominal muscles and pulled my hands down, and the two halves of the back rest parted as my head lowered to my knees. The further I pulled forward and down, the harder my crotch pushed forward against the raised hump in the pad. With each rep, my clit got more and more stimulated, until I began to feel an orgasm welling up inside me.

"That's it, Jade," Kate said, caressing my lower back from behind the machine. "You're doing great. Keep your back pressed against my hand and go as low as you can, bringing your elbows and knees together. Can you feel the burn?"

"Yes," I panted. "It feels good."

"Good. Just four more reps."

As I felt the pleasure continue building up between my legs, I had no intention of stopping at four reps. I pulled forward faster and lower, pressing my pussy harder against the pad each time.

"Uhnn," I groaned, nearing climax.

"Keep going, Jade," Kate encouraged me. "Press through the limit."

"Yes," I panted. "I can feel myself reaching the limit. Ohhh!" I moaned, feeling my orgasm pouring over me. On the last rep, I held the machine in the crunched position, pressing my cunt against the pad until my contractions ended, then I pulled back on the machine as the plates loudly fell together.

Kate smiled at me as she came back around to the front of the machine.

"Did you feel that in your core?" she said. "You did particularly well on this machine."

"Yes," I said. "I felt that *deep* in my core. Do you mind if I do another set?"

2

FEELING THE BURN

After my hot workout session with Kate, I immediately booked another personal training appointment. Even though she'd set me up with a full regimen of exercises, I liked having her push me to my limits. With her sexy body standing beside me, it definitely made me work harder. Not only did she boost my energy level, but she also represented the perfect figure that I could aspire to.

I wanted to go back for another session the next day, but Kate suggested I wait forty-eight hours to let my body rest and recover. She warned me that I'd likely experience some muscle aches in the areas we'd targeted, and the next morning I could barely pull myself out of bed. Which wasn't so much of a problem, since I languored for the first hour or two fantasizing about having her fuck me in every conceivable position.

By the second day, the aches were beginning to subside, and I was charged up for another intense training session. But if it was going to be anything like the last session, I figured I'd better wear something a little less revealing.

Although Kate didn't seem to mind, I definitely felt self-conscious about the wet spot showing in the crotch of my tights. I threw on some terrycloth sweats and a loose T-shirt, but dispensed with the bra and panties. Looking at myself in my dressing mirror, I nodded approvingly. I showed just enough curves to keep myself—and hopefully also Kate—turned on while I worked out.

When I got to the gym, Kate was waiting for me with my training chart on her clipboard. This time, she wore a form-fitting two-piece outfit that revealed most of her midsection. Below her truncated top, her toned stomach flexed with muscles and striations. I could see the faint outline of a six-pack, with a sexy indentation running down the center of her abdomen. Her tight leotards rested low on her hips, revealing a tantalizing patch of smooth, tanned skin below her navel, and the crest of her hip bones on either side.

The separated garments accentuated her hourglass figure, with her large, firm breasts swelling above her flared hips. Even with her legs straight together, I could see a small diamond-shaped patch of light emanating from the cleft at the top of her thighs. She couldn't have had more than five percent body fat anywhere on her body.

"How are you feeling today?" she said, stepping forward to greet me. "Any aches and pains after your first workout?"

"Oh yes," I said. "You weren't kidding about the next day training effect. I could barely walk yesterday."

"That's actually a good sign," she nodded. "There's two kinds of workout pain, and that's definitely the right kind. It means your muscles are breaking down and rebuilding stronger. Just like a broken bone, they heal back stronger and sturdier."

"That's good to know, because I think you almost broke me last time." I said, smiled coyly. "But I kind of liked it."

"Workouts produce an odd mixture of pleasure and pain. It's a lot of hard work, but the endorphins you produce from stressing your body give you a natural high."

"Well I definitely experienced a few highs," I said, remembering the intense orgasm I'd experienced on the ab crunch machine. "What have you got in store for me today?"

"I think you should stick to a balanced routine of stretching, weights, and cardio, but I'd like to mix up the exercises a little bit today. Besides keeping your body guessing what to expect next, it will give you more time to rest each set of muscles between sessions. Today, I want to work on your extremities, to boost your strength and stamina in some of the smaller muscles."

"Yes," I said, glancing again at the cleft at the top of Kate's thighs. "Let's definitely work on the extremities."

"Alright. Let's get you warmed up first with a little stretching."

Kate led me back to the stretching mat where she sat down in front of me and spread her legs.

"Spread your feet apart, then touch mine. We're going to hold each other's hands and pull each other to stretch our inner thighs."

"I like the sound of that," I said, smiling at Kate.

I reached out my hands and Kate clasped them firmly, then gently pulled me toward her. As she tensed her stomach muscles, the striations rippled across her abs.

"Uhnn," I grunted, feeling the pull in my hamstrings and adductors.

"Can you feel that?" Kate asked. "I'm going to hold you here for a moment, while you breathe slowly and try to relax your muscles."

After a few seconds, I could feel the tension begin to ebb in my legs, and Kate pulled me forward another few inches.

Each time she pulled me closer, she pushed my feet slightly further apart as my face got closer to her toned stomach and the bare skin below her navel. Just as I was getting tantalizingly close to her crotch, she eased up and suddenly sat forward.

"Now it's your turn to pull me toward you. This will stretch the top of your thighs and also strengthen your lower back and buttock muscles. Do the same thing I did—pulling me slowly forward until you feel the tension in my body.

I leaned back, pulling Kate's arms with me, and she flexed her body in a perfect V-shape, bobbing her head forward until her ponytail flopped down just in front of my crotch.

"Can you feel the stretch in your thighs?" Kate asked with her nose touching the mat.

"Among other places," I said.

We continued pushing and pulling each other for the next few minutes, pressing our legs further and further apart. Each time I pulled her forward, Kate's soft hair caressed the top of my mound as I unconsciously pushed my hips up in a fucking motion. By the time we finished the routine, my pussy was soaking wet, and I was glad I'd worn the heavy sweats.

"Okay," Kate said, standing up. "Let's work on loosening up your shoulders now. Extend your arm straight in front of you, then grab your elbow with your other hand and pull your arm slowly across your chest like this."

Kate demonstrated the movement as I watched her breasts mash together and press upward. I did the same, pretending to stretch my arm up and down as I rubbed the cotton fabric of my shirt against my bare nipples.

"Now the other side."

As I mirrored her technique, I couldn't take my eyes off her beautiful melons, wishing it were my face mashed up against them instead of her arm.

"Okay," she said. "This next stretch is a little more challenging. It's called the cow-face pose, and you should feel it under your arms and in your shoulder blades."

Kate lifted her arm over her head then reached behind her back with her other arm and joined her hands between her shoulder blades. I tried to copy her technique but grunted trying to touch my fingers.

"Don't worry if you can't join your hands together right away. As with our other stretches, just go as far as you can, then pause and breathe and try to push it a little further."

After a few more seconds of grunting and straining, I was finally able to touch my hands.

"Good," Kate said. "Now try to curl your fingers and pull your hands closer together. You should feel the stretch in your lats and deltoids."

"Oomph," I grimaced, feeling the strain in my back. "Now I see why they call this the cow-face pose."

"Well for the record," Kate said, "you don't look anything like a cow."

"Um—thank you," I said, running my eyes up and down Kate's taut figure. "I don't think you look remotely like any barn animal either."

"All right then," Kate chuckled. "Let's go find some new pastures to graze in. I think we need some fresh material to get charged up on."

She led me to the back wall where a bunch of jocks were lifting free weights in front of a long mirror. Kate positioned a bench in front of the mirror then lifted two twenty-pound dumbbells off the rack and sat down on the end of the bench. She lowered the weights behind her head until her arms were in a ninety-degree angle, then she raised them straight up.

"This exercise will tighten up the underside of your upper arms. Try to keep your elbows stationary beside your ears as you lift the weights straight up and down. I'll stand behind you to watch your form."

She motioned for me to sit as she had on the bench, then she removed two five-pound dumbbells and placed them in my outstretched hands.

"That's only a *quarter* of what you were doing," I said. "When can I expect to reach your level?"

"I've been training pretty intensely my entire adult life. If you get there much quicker than me, I'm going to be a little envious."

"You mean I have to wait *fifteen years* to start looking like you?"

"It won't take that long," Kate chuckled. "Remember, fitness is a journey, not a destination. It should only take a few months for you to start noticing some significant changes."

Kate stepped behind me and placed her hands around my elbows.

"Now, lower the weights slowly until your arms are in a ninety-degree angle."

Feeling Kate's bare hands close to my chest sent a chill down my spine, and I began pumping the weights up and down quickly.

"Slow down, girl," Kate admonished. "This isn't a race. Slower is always better. There's less chance of getting a muscle strain, and it places more even force throughout the entire range of motion."

"Right," I said, staring at her rack sitting just above my head. "Slower is better."

By the time I finished ten reps, my tricep muscles were burning, and I rested the dumbbells on my thighs.

"Good job," Kate said. "Just two more sets."

I looked at her like she was crazy, and she simply nodded.

"No pain, no gain," she smiled.

"You're a cruel woman," I said, pushing the weights back over my head.

As I began lowering and lifting the dumbbells, I noticed Kate's gaze drifting to my chest as my loose breasts swayed under the thin cotton fabric of my T-shirt. Within a few seconds, my nipples had hardened, producing two noticeable bumps in my shirt. I was happy to see I wasn't the only one attracted by nice tits, and I proudly lifted my chest, pressing my breasts further forward and higher.

"All right," Kate said after I finished the third set. "Let's get a pump going to your antagonist muscles. It's always good to keep your strength balanced on both sides of your body to avoid injury and to build a symmetrical shape. Now we're going to work on your biceps."

"Biceps?" I said. "Aren't those just for *guys*? I thought you said you weren't going to make me look like Arnold Schwarzenegger."

"Not to worry. We're going to use light weights. I promise you won't bulk up. Do you think *I* look like Arnold Schwarzenegger?"

"God, no," I said, admiring her slender but strong arms. "You look more like an Amazon. A very *sexy* Amazon. If this will make me look like you, I'm all in."

"Follow me then. Let's *pump you up!*" she said, feigning a German accent.

I was beginning to enjoy my playful banter with Kate.

The more time I spent with her, the more infatuated I became.

She walked up to the weight rack and picked up two five-pound dumbbells. Then she stepped back a couple of feet and began swinging her hands up and down in alternating arcs. As she lifted the weights, I stared at her arm muscles flexing with sinewy firmness. I wanted to jump up on her shoulders and clamp my legs around her head while she held me up with her strong arms as I ground my pussy into her face.

"Jade?" Kate said, running her hand in front of my glazed eyes. "Are you still with me? It's your turn now."

"Yes," I murmured, snapping out of my daydream. "I was just concentrating on your—*technique*."

Kate passed me the five-pound weights and as I began to pump the dumbbells up and down, she moved behind me and gripped my shoulders to keep my body from swaying. Every time she placed her hands on me, I fantasized about her touching my more private parts.

Looking out the corner of my eyes, I noticed a few muscle jocks leering at us from the other side of the gym.

"Do you ever provide *private* lessons?" I asked.

"You mean outside the gym?"

"Yes. It can be a bit disconcerting doing all this intimate lifting with so many eyes on you."

"I can do outcalls," Kate nodded. "But it's a little tougher to achieve the same intensity without access to all this specialized equipment. Do you have a suitable area of your home in which you can work out?"

I paused for a moment, contemplating my options.

"I could probably clear a space. But I don't have any equipment. What about *your* place? I'm guessing you have a more complete setup."

"I have a small studio with a few free weights and cardio machines," Kate said. "We could create a workable routine just using your own body weight."

"That sounds very liberating. Can we try that next time?"

"Of course. Let's finish up here though today. Don't mind those muscleheads. They're harmless."

As I continued my bicep set, Kate's grip on my shoulders tightened, until her fingertips pressed into the side of my breasts. Whether she was just trying to steady my swaying body or she was turned on by my invitation for a private get together, was unclear. Either way, her firm grip got me even more worked up, and I hammered out three sets before realizing how much my arms were burning.

"Doesn't that feel good?" Kate said, motioning to my pumped-up biceps.

I looked in the mirror and flexed my arms, admiring the new curves produced by the opposing arms exercises.

"Yes," I nodded. "I like where this is going."

"Okay," she said. "Just two more exercises. Let's see if we can finish up on another high today."

"Are you taking me back to the ab crunch machine?" I asked, feeling my pussy pulsing between my legs. "Cause that thing has a *special* effect on me."

"Not today. But I have something you might like just as much."

She led me over to a weight machine shaped like a gynecologist's chair. Leg rests extended out from the machine in a V-shape, with hand rests beside the padded seat. Kate sat in the machine and adjusted a handle beside the seat to spread her legs wide apart. As she pulled her legs together, the weight stack on the front of the machine began to rise.

"This will tighten and strengthen your groin muscles," she said. "It's another good one for enhancing your sex life.

Keeps everything nice and tight down there. You never know when you might need to wrap your legs around something—"

"Indeed," I said, recognizing another dark patch forming in the crotch of her tights. There was only one place I wanted to wrap my legs around at this moment.

When she finished demonstrating the machine, Kate lowered the weight and asked me to do a few sets. I pulled my legs together and grunted from the tightness in my groin muscles. But within four or five reps, I was getting the hang of the exercise as I began to feel a more pleasurable sensation between my legs.

"That's it, Jade," Kate said. "Spread your legs nice and slow. This is one muscle you definitely don't want to pull."

"Not *this* way at least," I said, smiling at Kate.

As I continued fanning my legs in and out, I fantasized about having her face buried in my pussy as I wrapped my legs around her head.

"I can see what you mean, though. This exercise is definitely very—*invigorating*."

After two more sets, we moved to the adjacent machine which focused on our outer thighs and hips. By the time I finished the requisite three sets, the terrycloth lining of my sweats was already soaked through again. But this time, Kate rarely took her gaze away from the wet patch between my legs.

"I knew you'd like these ones," she smiled. "It looks like you're just about ready for the big finish."

"Yes," I said. "I need to finish soon. All this flexing and straining in my groin area is getting me pretty worked up."

"Let's see if we can take you to another new peak," Kate said, smiling.

She led me to a tall weight rack with padded shoulder

rests and an elevated foot rest.

"This one works on your lower legs. It will give you a nice pleasing shape to your calves."

"*Lower* legs?" I said. "I was kind of hoping we'd finish with another core exercise."

"I think you might find this one just as satisfying," she said. "It's a bit more interactive. But this time, I want *you* to go first. I'm going to stand behind you to guide your movement. Then we'll switch and you can return the favor."

I pinched my eyebrows, intrigued by Kate's cryptic description.

"Okay, but how does it work?"

"Place the balls of your feet on the edge of the elevated foot rest, then rest your shoulders under the padded supports and lift your heels as high as you can with a straight body."

As I began to raise my heels and lift the weight stack, Kate pressed her body against mine to keep my body straight. When I lowered my heels, she pushed her hips against my ass. I smiled as I looked around the gym, glad that this machine was nestled in the corner behind a tall rack of barbells. For the next few minutes, Kate and I would have almost complete privacy.

"That's it," Kate said, pressing her mound against my ass. Her hands gripped the sides of my hips as she pulled herself against me. "Keep doing what you're doing. Up and down—nice and slow."

A flush began to form on Kate's cheeks with each lowering of my hips, and I began to push my ass into her as she tilted her crotch up to meet me. Even though she'd intentionally set the weight on the stack low so I wouldn't exhaust too quickly, by the twentieth rep or so I began to feel my calves burning.

"That's good, Jade," Kate said, exhaling heavily against the back of my loose shirt. "Try to push out five or ten more reps. We're almost there."

I noticed her breathing had picked up in intensity and her face now had a full flush.

"Two more, Jade," she panted. "Push it."

Suddenly, Kate pressed her face against my back and I felt her body shudder against my ass. I held my heels up in an extended position, pressing my butt against her pussy, until I felt her grip loosen against my hips.

"That was very good," she panted. "You really pushed through your limits that time. Now let's switch positions and see if you can stimulate some *other* parts of your body while I do all the work."

I looked into Kate's eyes and smiled.

"Do you need a moment to recover?"

"I'll be fine," she said, glancing at the wet patch in the front of my sweat pants. "*You're* the one who needs attention right now. Stand behind me and guide me as I guided you. Let's see if we can finish with an extra-big pump."

"I like the sound of that," I said, caressing Kate's hips as she stepped in front of me. "Just don't put too much weight on the stack. I don't want you to get exhausted before I do."

Kate stepped on the foot rest and playfully pressed her ass against me as she dipped her shoulders under the supports. I moved in close behind her and looked around the room to make sure nobody else was watching. When she straightened her body and lifted her heels, I felt her ass tighten and flex against my stomach. I placed my hands around her waist, pressing my thumbs into her rock-hard butt. When she lowered her heels, she paused at the bottom and shimmied her glutes across my mound.

"Yes," I purred. "You have such great form, Kate. Don't

stop. Show me how to perform this exercise properly. Nice and slow..."

I smiled at Kate in the mirror in front of us as she lifted herself up and lowered herself slowly, sensuously sliding her ass down the front of my sweats. The coarse lining of my pants rubbed against my clit, like a French tickler.

"Uhnnn," I moaned. "That feels good. Pump that weight. Fuck me with your tight ass."

There was no point withholding any further pretense. We both knew what we were doing, and I had no intention of disguising the effect she had on me. As she continued sliding up and down the front of my body, my hands migrated further and further toward the front of Kate's leotard, until my fingertips probed the cleft between her legs.

"Yes, Jade," she panted. "I'm beginning to feel the burn. Let's push through our limits together this time."

We pressed our bodies tighter together, and as Kate rubbed her body over my pussy, I diddled her clit with my two hands.

"Yes, Jade," Kate grunted. "It's coming. I'm reaching my peak. Oh, fuck!"

Kate's buttocks suddenly began vibrating against my mound, and I pressed my clit into her hard ass as I gushed into my terrycloth sweat pants.

"Oh God," I panted. "Fuck me, Kate! Fuck me with your sweet ass!"

I gripped her pelvis tightly as I thrashed against her butt, hissing against her back, trying to suppress my exploding pleasure. For the next twenty seconds, we spasmed against one another, savoring a quiet and intense simultaneous orgasm.

3

PUSHING THE LIMITS

After my second exciting workout with Kate, she gave me her personal contact information and we scheduled a private session for later in the week. Normally, she preferred to visit her clients at their residence for outcalls, but in my case she was willing to make an exception and meet me at her home.

As with my first training session, I was sore in the new muscles we'd targeted, but especially so in my abs, which had gotten a particularly intense workout while grinding my hips against her ass during the calf raise exercise. If it was her intent to use sexual gratification as an incentive to make me work harder, I could only imagine what she had in store for me during our third session.

On Saturday morning, I followed the directions to her home and at eleven o'clock I tapped on the front door of her house. When she opened the door, I was disappointed to see her wearing a full-body sweatsuit. Knowing nobody would be watching us today, I'd worn my skimpiest two-piece yoga outfit. I no longer had any reservations about Kate seeing first-hand the sexual effects her workouts were having on my body.

"Good morning, Jade," she said, inviting me inside.

"You have a beautiful home," I said, looking around her tastefully appointed house. "Thanks for inviting me. I was beginning to feel a bit self-conscious with all those mirrors and prying eyes surrounding us at the gym."

"That's the problem when you have two attractive, toned women working out around all those muscleheads," Kate nodded. "It's like they'd never seen a fit woman before. Today, I just want you to relax and let yourself go. I've got a special routine worked up for you."

Kate motioned to her kitchen at the opposite end of the hall.

"Can I get you something to drink? How about a nice healthy smoothie?"

"That would be lovely."

Kate led me to her kitchen and suggested I sit on a stool beside the island while she prepared the refreshment. As she loaded an assortment of fruits and vegetables into her blending machine, I watched her round ass bend and flex in her sweats. When the machine finished its cycle, she poured the mixture into two tall glasses then sat beside me at the island. I took a sip of the dark green concoction and puckered my lips from the bitter taste.

"Do you drink this stuff *every* day?" I asked.

"Pretty much," she said, "especially before or after a training session. There's lots of good vitamins and protein in there. Helps to rebuild your muscles after a workout. I'm guessing from your cow-face that you're not digging it?"

"Sorry to make light of your culinary skills," I chuckled. "I'm sure it's very good for me. No pain, no gain—right?"

"Unfortunately, that's the way it is with most good things

if life," Kate nodded. "You need to make certain sacrifices in order to achieve your goals."

"Speaking of sacrifices," I said, peering at her heavy sweatsuit. "I have to admit I'm a little disappointed that you're covering up your pretty body today. Seeing your magnificent figure really gave me the motivation to push harder."

Kate smiled as she glanced at my firm breasts in my tight yoga top.

"Don't worry," she said. "I have some interesting ideas for pushing your limits today. I think we'll get plenty of opportunities to see our muscles pumping up close today. Finish your smoothie, and I'll show you what I mean."

Kate's suggestion that I'd see more of her body once we started working out was all the encouragement that I needed. I gulped down the rest of my smoothie then followed her downstairs to her finished walkout basement. When we got to the bottom of the stairs, I looked around the expansive room and nodded in appreciation. The entire lower level was filled with an assortment of free weights, training mats, and cardio machines. Three sides of the room were lined with floor-to-ceiling mirrors, while the side facing her fenced-in yard had tall windows streaming in the morning sunlight.

"Wow," I said, widening my eyes in wonder. "This is quite the exercise studio. No wonder you're in such great shape. I'd want to workout out here *every day* I had this setup. It's almost as big as the gym!"

"Not quite," Kate said, "but thank you. It's taken a while to equip, but I have to admit, I've got no excuse to miss a workout with just about everything I need so readily available."

"Where shall we begin?" I asked, looking at all the gleaming equipment.

"Let's start on the stretching mat. I've designed most of the exercises using only your own body weight. Besides enabling you to do them away from the gym, they're also a little more *interactive*."

"Interactive sounds good," I said, smiling at Kate.

She led me to a large padded mat near the back wall then paused, looking at me in the mirror.

"The first thing I think we should do is disrobe," she said. "Besides giving you a little extra incentive to push out that extra rep, it will give me a chance to see first-hand the effect each exercise is having on your body."

My eyes flung open as my pussy twitched between my legs.

"Completely?" I said.

"You said seeing more of my body made you work harder, didn't you? By extension, the more we reveal, I'm guessing the harder you'll work."

As much as I wanted to see Kate naked, the thought of working out in the buff felt strange.

"Maybe," I said. "But it could also be a little distracting—"

"Let me worry about keeping you focused on the exercises. You just concentrate on following my instructions. Are you comfortable with this idea?"

"Are you kidding me?" I said. "I've been undressing you with my eyes from the moment we first met."

"Alright then," Kate said, unzipping the front of her sweat top. "Let's do this."

She lowered her zipper all the way, then pulled her jacket off her back and threw it in the corner of the mat. She wasn't wearing anything underneath, and I gasped when I saw her large breasts resting on her chest. They had to be D-cup sized at least, yet they sat firm and high on her chest. They were perfectly round, with a sharp crease from her defined pec muscles separating them in the middle. Her large pink, medallion-sized areolas were punctuated with thick nipples extending almost a full inch from the surface of her skin . My pussy throbbed as I felt my tights moistening in excitement.

"Holy shit, girl," I said. "Are those things *real*? They look like something straight out of a Playboy centerfold."

"One hundred percent natural," Kate smiled. "I was blessed with large breasts from a young age. They were even bigger than this before I started working out. That was one of my primary motivations for getting in shape and reducing my body fat. I was always self-conscious about the size of my breasts."

"Well you shouldn't be," I said, shaking my head as the wet patch widened in my crotch. "They're absolutely magnificent. Most women would give their right arm to have a rack like yours."

"Maybe," Kate said. "But not everybody likes big boobs. They can be a little annoying when I'm exercising, particularly when I'm on the treadmill."

"I bet. You could take an *eye* out with those things if you aren't careful."

"I'm sure you know what I'm talking about," Kate smiled. "You've got a pretty healthy set yourself, Jade. Speaking of which, isn't it time for you to do a little show and tell yourself?"

"Oh—sorry," I said, hooking my fingers under the hem of my yoga top. "I just wanted to soak up your body for a few seconds."

I pulled my shirt over my head then threw it on top of

Kate's sweatshirt. As I stood facing Kate with my naked breasts, my body trembled in excitement.

"Perfect C's," Kate said, nodding appreciatively. "I suspect that's more like what most women aspire to. I don't think you need any help there."

"Maybe not," I said, running my eyes down the length of Kate's body. "It's the *rest* of my body that needs work."

"Let's see what we have to work with the rest of the way then," she said, suddenly pulling her sweat pants down to the floor and throwing them in the pile.

Once again, she was completely naked under her pants, and my mouth gaped open when I saw her exposed lower body. Her mound was shaved completely bald, and her hips swelled in a sexy hourglass shape with exposed hipbones framed by abdominal ligaments angling toward her pussy. Her thighs flared in a gentle muscular arc over diamond-shaped calves and narrow ankles. Her entire body looked like it had been carved from a slab of marble.

"You've got to be kidding me," I panted. "You look like a Greek Goddess. I just want to eat you up."

"We might be able to arrange that a little later," Kate said, staring at the giant wet patch that had formed in the crotch of my leggings. "First let's get you out of the rest of your clothes. You look a little uncomfortable in those wet leggings."

"What if I leak all over your beautiful workout studio? Won't it bother you if I soil your clean stretching mat?"

"Not at all," Kate said. "It will just add some helpful lubrication to some of the exercises I've got planned. Let's get started by celebrating our mutual figures. I want you to start by turning around and spreading your legs about two feet apart. I'll stand behind you, then we'll bend at the waist and view ourselves between our legs."

"I like the sound of that," I said, quickly turning around and bending over.

But when I peered through my legs, I saw that Kate had moved closer to me, and I struggled to tilt my head far enough down to see her full back side. As she started to bend forward, the muscles in her calves and the back of her thighs rippled in sexy striations. She smiled at me when me made eye contact, but she was too close for me to see her upturned ass and exposed pussy.

"No fair!" I protested, straining to look further up her legs.

"I *told* you I was going to make this a little more interesting today," she said. "If you want to see more of my naked body, you're going to have to work for it."

I groaned, feeling my hamstring muscles straining as I struggled to push myself further down to give me a better viewing angle.

"Don't push it too fast," Kate said. "We've still got a long workout ahead of us. I don't want you to hurt yourself before you have a chance to do some closer contact activities."

She wiggled her feet away from me a few inches, allowing me to see a few inches higher up her thighs, but her honeypot was still just barely out of view. I placed my hands around my ankles and pulled my body a few inches lower, until I could see the bottom of her slit. Kate quickly scurried closer to me, reducing my field of vision.

"You little tease," I growled, frustrated by my inability to get a clear look at her cunny.

"I never said this was going to be *easy*," Kate said. "The main purpose of a personal trainer is to push you further than you would by yourself."

As I gawked at Kate's shapely legs, I could feel my juices running down the insides of my thighs.

"Yeah, well if you keep teasing me like this, I may need to take matters into my own hands pretty soon."

"There'll be plenty of time for that later. You're not allowed to touch *anything* until I give my permission. Take a deep breath and exhale slowly. Feel the pressure in your muscles relax, then you'll be able to stretch a little lower."

I did as Kate instructed, and as I felt my breasts press against the front of my thighs, my field of vision rose another two inches up the back of Kate's legs.

"Almost there, Jade," Kate said, wiggling a couple of inches closer to me. "Pause and relax. Just a couple more inches..."

I closed my eyes and concentrated on my breathing as the pressure in my hamstrings slowly abated. When I opened them again, Kate's tight box sat directly in front of me between her splayed legs. The cheeks of her muscular buttocks cupped her bare vulva like a catcher's mitt, her puffy lips spreading apart sensuously to reveal her dark glistening slit.

"Fuck yes," I purred, when I saw her exposed snatch. "Even your pussy is perfectly tight and ripped. Why am I not surprised? Come a little closer and let me feel your ass press against mine. I want to fuck that sweet, sexy pussy."

Kate smiled at me as she licked her lips.

"You've got a sexy kitty too, Jade. We'll have plenty of opportunity to join our bodies soon enough. For now, I want you to hold that position while you stretch your hamstrings just a little longer."

"God damn, girl" I hissed. "You weren't kidding when you said you had a special plan for pushing me past my limits today."

"You haven't seen anything yet," Kate said. "We're just getting started."

Kate suddenly stood up and turned around as I lifted myself back up slowly.

"Now we're going to work on another part of your body," she said. "This will give us a chance to admire a different piece of our anatomy. I want you to lie face up on the mat, with your body in a straight position and your legs together."

I pinched my eyebrows and looked at Kate quizzically as I lowered myself to the mat as she instructed. Then she straddled my legs and began to walk on her hands and knees up my body.

"Yes please," I said. "While you're down there, would you mind—"

"Shush, little girl," she said. "I have something *else* in mind."

She crawled two more feet up my body, then stretched her legs out behind her and lifted her body up on her palms and the balls of her feet. As she stared directly down onto my face, she smiled at me slyly, then lowered her body until her breasts almost touched mine. Then she raised herself back up until her arms were straight and repeated the sequence two more times.

"This is what I call a reverse bench press," she said. "It works the same muscles on the back of your arms and the front of your chest, but in a more fun and interesting way. We're going to switch positions in a moment, and I want you to mimic my movement, lowering your body with a straight back as far as you can without touching me. Do as many reps as you can until you reach exhaustion."

"Without *touching*?" I said. "Where's the fun in that? I thought you were going to use your sexy body as an incentive to push me further. If I can't touch you, where's my motivation?"

"That's the whole point of the exercise," Kate smiled. "I'm withholding the touching part until the last to encourage you to work harder. If you're a good girl and you do everything the way I tell you, there'll be a nice little reward at the end."

"There better be," I said. "Because if my muscles don't give out first, surely my willpower will."

"Get on top of me and fantasize about what you want to do to me later. That should give you plenty of motivation to finish your exercises."

Kate rolled over on the mat beside me and straightened her body out as I had. Then I straddled her hips and looked into her eyes mischievously.

"Now that I've got you where I want you, what makes you think I won't just take advantage of you right here?"

"Do you really think you can take me that easily?" Kate taunted. "Keep your dick in your pants, girl. Don't make me teach you a different kind of lesson today. Now straighten out your body and pump out some push-ups."

"Yes master," I said, winking at Kate.

As I lowered my body, I struggled to keep my body straight, with my arms shaking from the force of my weight levitating over Kate. As our bodies came closer and closer together, I peered down to see my nipples mere inches away from Kate's inflamed nubs. Momentarily overcome with passion, my arms suddenly became weak, and our nipples touched.

"No contact!" Kate admonished. "If you can't hold yourself in the lower position, straighten out your arms and rest for longer at the top. Use our nipples as a guide. I want you to get as close to me as possible without actually touching. Now—straighten back up!"

I did as Kate instructed and paused with my arms in a locked position above her. My heavy breathing blew loose strands of hair at the sides of her head.

"Okay," Kate said. "Try it again. This time, get as close as you dare—but no touching."

"You're *killing* me!" I protested, half from exhaustion and half from sexual frustration.

I lowered myself again, peering between my tits to get as close to Kate's nipples without actually making contact.

"That's it, babe," Kate encouraged. "Lower those tender melons. Let me see your hard nipples lining up with mine. Feel the electricity between us, like a spark between two terminals. Feel the burn in your arms and your stomach while you hold the position."

"I feel it," I panted, dripping from my soaking pussy onto her upper thighs. "Not only there. But I can't hold it much longer—"

"Lift yourself back up into the extended position," she said. "Just two more reps."

I looked at Kate and shook my head.

"I don't think I can do it. Not without collapsing onto you. And if that means ruining my chances with you later, I don't want to risk it."

"Alright," Kate said, peering up at me. "I'm going to give you a little break. Rest your knees on the floor while you do the last few reps. That will lower the load on your arms and make it easier for you to do the push-ups. Continue."

I lowered my knees to the mat beside Kate's hips and immediately felt half the weight release from my arms.

"That's better," I puffed.

"Good. You should be able to do *four* more reps now with

the lower weight. Now bring those titties back down to Momma."

I lowered my body, concentrating on the narrowing distance between our breasts, but I hadn't calculated on the effect my kneeling position would have nearer our midsection. Just as I was inches away from touching Kate's nipples, my sopping pussy rubbed against Kate's mound.

"Oh *Gawd*," I moaned, as another surge of wetness seeped out of my pussy onto Kate's abdomen.

"Keep your body straight!" Kate ordered. "Lift your hips. No touching is allowed."

"I'm *trying* to keep my body straight," I protested, furrowing my brow. "It's just that our hips are closer together this way..."

"Fair enough," Kate nodded. "Next rep, lift your hips just high enough to keep from touching me down below too. That will help tighten up your stomach at the same time. Now—three more reps."

"At this rate, I'm not going to have any energy left for the fun part at the end," I panted, lifting myself back up.

"Don't worry," Kate said, smiling into my eyes. "We'll rotate the exercises so you don't exhaust any one part before you run out of steam. Now finish up. I've got something even more exciting lined up for you next."

I managed to eke out three more reps with my hips in an elevated position, then I rolled over and collapsed onto the mat, massaging my aching arm muscles.

"C'mon, girl," Kate said, extending a hand and pulling me back up onto my feet. "Let's give those arms a rest and begin to work on your lower body. I've got something very special in store for you with our next exercise."

She led me over to the corner where a long, padded bench rested in front of another panel of mirrors. She straddled the bench facing the mirror and demonstrated a deep squat, lowering herself up and down just far enough to not touch the bench with her ass and pussy.

"Your turn," she said, stepping away from the bench.

"That doesn't look like all that much fun," I said. "We already did this one in our first workout together."

"You'll see," Kate said, smiling at my coyly. "We're going to mix it up soon enough."

"No weight?" I said, touching my hand to my shoulders.

Kate shook her head.

"We're going for more reps this time. You'll feel the burn as intensely as before, if not more so. Just remember as with the pushups, to go down as far as you can without touching the pad."

"You're a cruel woman, Kate," I said, straddling the bench.

"Hopefully you won't think so by the time we finish. Now let's pump those legs."

As I began to lower myself over the bench, I watched myself in the mirror directly in front of me. Each time I lowered my pussy to within an inch of the bench, I could see my tingling clit poking out between my legs, begging to be caressed by the soft vinyl padding.

"Are you sure I can't touch the bench, even just lightly?" I pleaded. "I promise not to rest my weight. I just want a little stimulation down there. All this near-contact is killing me."

"Not yet," Kate said. "Do ten more reps, then we'll see if we can find a way to make it more stimulating for you."

I hammered out the ten reps faster than I'd ever done before. By the time I finished, another pool of clear liquid had pooled on the bench directly under my hips.

"You were right," I said, massaging the front of my thighs.

"I feel that in my quads just as much as last time. But I don't know how many more of these I can do."

Kate looked at me with a sinister grin.

"Oh, I think you've got a few more left in you," she said. "You just need a little extra motivation."

She turned around and reached into a dresser drawer beside the bench and pulled out a long, fat, realistic dildo. It had a suction cup on the bottom, and Kate rubbed the cup against my juices on the bench, then pressed it firmly down against the fabric.

I looked up at her with wide eyes.

"You're not actually expecting me to do more of these without touching *that* thing also?"

"This time I'm going to allow you to touch it," she said. "In fact, *more* than just touch it. I want you to lower yourself fully down and fuck the dildo by pumping up and down on it. The only catch is you can't sit all the way down to rest your legs. I think you'll find the cock gives you plenty of motivation to do a few extra reps and get an extra long pump."

"Holy fuck," I said, shaking my head at Kate. "You really *have* been dreaming up all the ways you can torture me today, haven't you?"

"You said you wanted to take it to the next level. You must have known that by coming to my place, we were going to get a lot more interactive with our exercises than before."

"Yes," I said. "But I hoped it would be more interactive with *you*, not some fake plastic dick."

"We'll get there soon enough," Kate said. "This is just a warmup for the final act. Now get down on that cock and see if you can reach a new peak."

Looking at Kate's beautiful naked body standing before me in the mirror, I didn't need any further encouragement. At this point, I would have fucked just about any object she placed in front of me. I slowly lowered my ass over the bench until I hovered a mere inch over the tip of the erect cock, then I looked at Kate in the mirror and she nodded. I lowered myself another couple of inches and moaned as the thick dildo spread my pussy apart. I sat down a little lower, feeling the cock fill me up until my ass almost touched the bench.

"Do I have come all the way back up?" I asked, looking at Kate in the mirror.

"Only if you want to. But I think you'll enjoy it more if you do a bunch of mini-reps with the cock embedded inside you. Just remember not to rest your weight at any time on the bench."

As I began to fuck the dildo up and down with my pussy, I could feel my thighs beginning to burn. I was just about to stand back up to take the pressure off my legs when I saw Kate place her hand between her legs and begin to finger herself. That encouraged me to keep myself squatted over the dildo, and we began to moan together as we watched each other in the mirror. As we both watched the giant cock emerging and disappearing into my snatch, I began to feel my climax stirring inside me.

"Fuck, Kate," I said. "This feels good, but I don't know how much longer I can continue. My legs are burning so bad."

"Just a few more reps, Jade," she said. "I can see you're so close. I'm going to try to come with you. Fuck that cock with everything you've got."

Seeing Kate moaning as she watched me suddenly gave me a second wind, and I began humping the dildo harder and faster. Within a few moments, my orgasm poured over me.

"Yes, Kate!" I screamed. "I'm cumming!"

As Kate watched me gushing all over the cock and the bench from my powerful orgasm, she suddenly hunched over in a series of jerking spasms.

"Fuck, yes," she groaned. "That's so hot. Fuck that big cock, Jade."

Thankfully, my orgasm was over within a few seconds, and I quickly raised myself up over my quaking legs. Kate moved forward to hold me, and we melded into each other's arms as we came down from our highs.

"Thank you for letting me touch it this time," I panted in her ear. "I really needed that. It's a good thing you saved this one for last, because I'm really spend now. But I was really hoping to feel you—"

"We're not done yet," Kate said. "Lie down on the stretching mat and relax for a moment. I have one last little exercise that I think you might find a last boost the energy to perform."

As we lay down on the mat beside each other, Kate rolled onto her side and kissed me gently. I pushed my body toward her and pressed our breasts and hips together, thankful we finally had a moment to revel in each other's bodies.

"Whoa, girl," she said, pulling away a few inches. "You've got to *earn* the final reward, remember? Working out was never meant to be easy."

"What the fuck?" I said. "But I thought—"

"I'm going to let you touch me soon enough," she smiled. "I just want you to get a bit more of a workout while you do it."

I looked at Kate and shook my head.

"Are you *always* all work and no play? Can't I ever just have a little fun with you?"

"We can do that when I'm off the clock," she said. "You've still got ten more minutes left in your workout."

"I can't imagine what else you could possibly want me to do," I said, exhaling heavily. "Haven't I pretty much exhausted every muscle in my body?"

Kate lifted herself up on one elbow and ran her fingers through my hair.

"Remember when I said it's important to work your muscles in pairs? We're going to finish up by working the agonist muscle to your quads, which is your hamstrings. But this time, I promise we'll have more fun doing it."

"As long as I can *touch* you," I said, "I don't care what kind of position you put me in."

"Good. Then lie down on the mat and lift your right leg into a ninety-degree angle. I'm going to lie facing you and do the same while we hold hands. You might need to crunch your stomach a little to pull far enough down to reach me."

Kate shimmied her body on the mat toward me until the right sides of our asses were touching each other, then she hooked the back of her right thigh behind mine. She reached out her hands, and I pulled forward to clasp them. Then she gripped me tightly and began pushing her leg toward me.

"Try to resist my movement and push back against me," she said. "See if you can oppose my force with an equal force. This exercise not only helps to strengthen your hamstrings, but it makes for a great tummy workout too."

I grunted as I pushed my thigh back toward her while gripping her hands to maintain pressure. Kate resisted my force, then pushed my knee back all the way up onto my breast.

"I'm not as strong as you," I protested. "I can't push as hard as you can."

"Don't worry about that," she said, peering over her shoulder at my splayed pussy. "Just push as hard as you can, feeling the pressure in your hamstrings and glutes."

I peered up at Kate and saw her glancing at my exposed snatch.

"You *like* that, don't you?" I said, feeling my juices running down the crack of my ass. "This is just another excuse to look at my wet pussy again, isn't it?"

"Yes," she said. "Not to mention your pretty little rosebud. Now push. Try to resist me!"

I grunted as I pushed my leg back toward her, and we see-sawed back and forth until the moisture emanating from both of our slits made us slide closer together. Suddenly, our pussies were directly touching, and I could feel Kate's ass rubbing up against mine. I spread my legs further apart and pulled myself up a few inches to peer at her between my legs. As Kate did the same, our hips tilted down until our clits touched.

"Oh God, Kate," I moaned. "Fuck me with your pussy. I want to cum all over your beautiful ass."

"Uhnnn," Kate grunted. "Lift yourself up higher, Jade. I want to see your pretty tits while I fuck you."

I pulled harder on Kate's hands, lifting myself into an elevated crunch position, and began pumping myself harder against her vulva. Within a few minutes, I began to feel an equally intense burn in my abdominal muscles and my pussy.

"I feel the burn, Kate," I panted. "Come with me. I don't know how much longer I can last. I'm getting close."

"Yes, Jade," Kate said. "Just a few more reps. Pump my

pussy with your wet cunt. I want to feel you cum all over me."

Her words soon pushed me over the top, and as we thrashed against each another's pussies, we screamed out loud, climaxing in blissful union. As I pulled myself forward to watch our cunts gnashing together, suddenly Kate squirted her juices through her tight slit, spraying her cum all over my tits and face.

"Fuckkkk, Jade!" she grunted, spraying her juices in a wide arc all over my torso. "You're an excellent trainee," she hissed. "We're going to have to make this a regular part of our routine."

"Yes, Kate," I panted. "You really know how to push me past my limits."

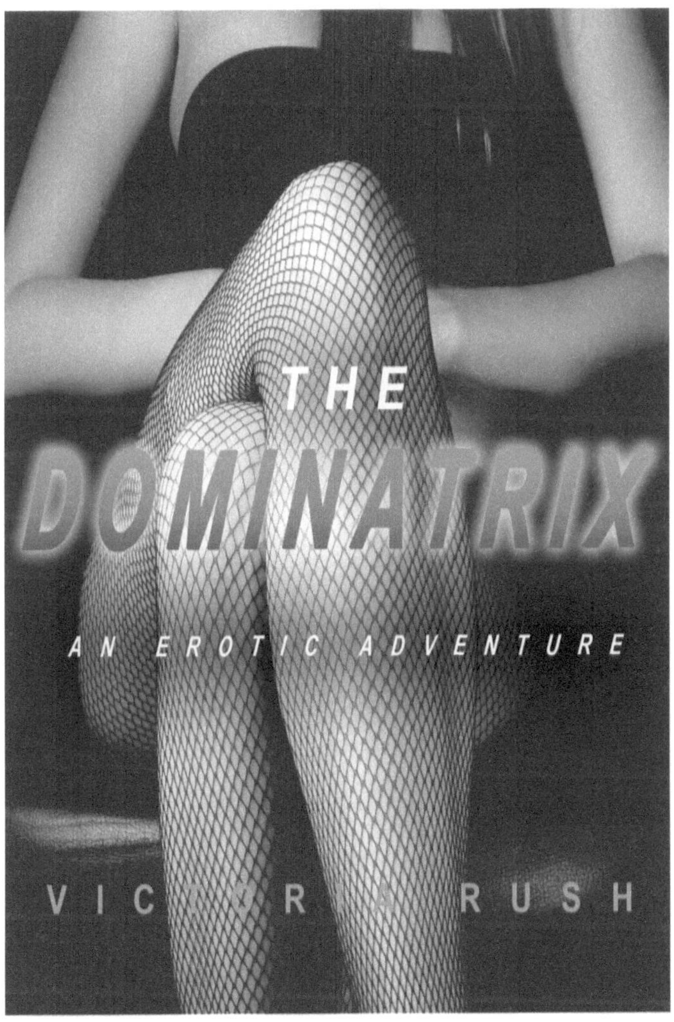

Sometimes it takes a little kink to break out of your usual routine...

Everyone's an exhibitionist in disguise...

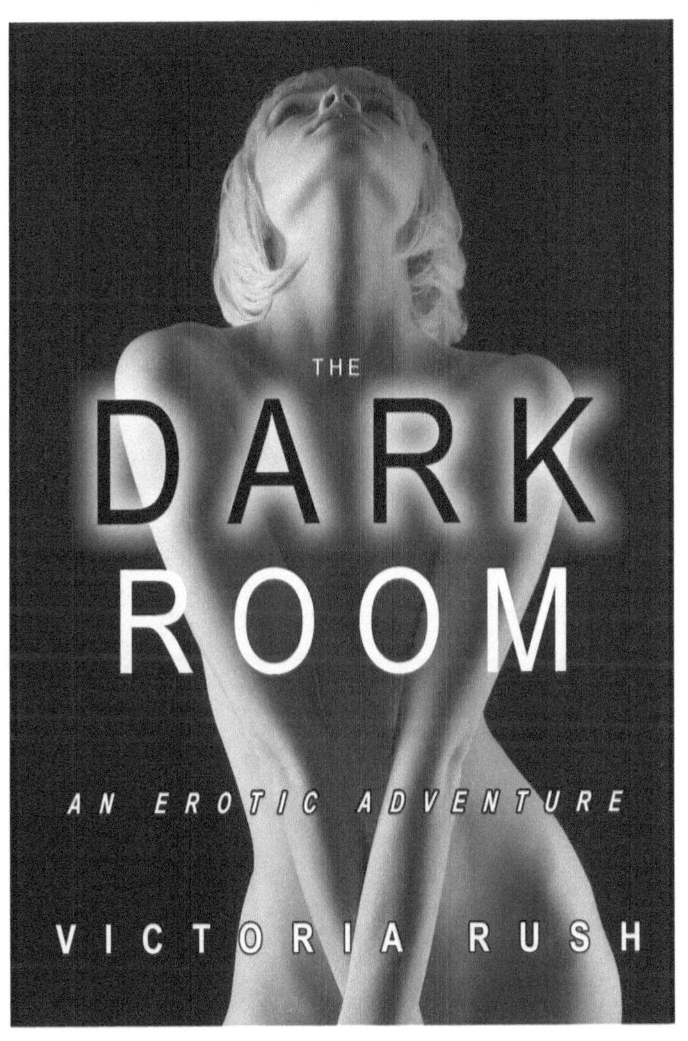

Everything's sexier in the dark...

Mula Bandha is for lovers...

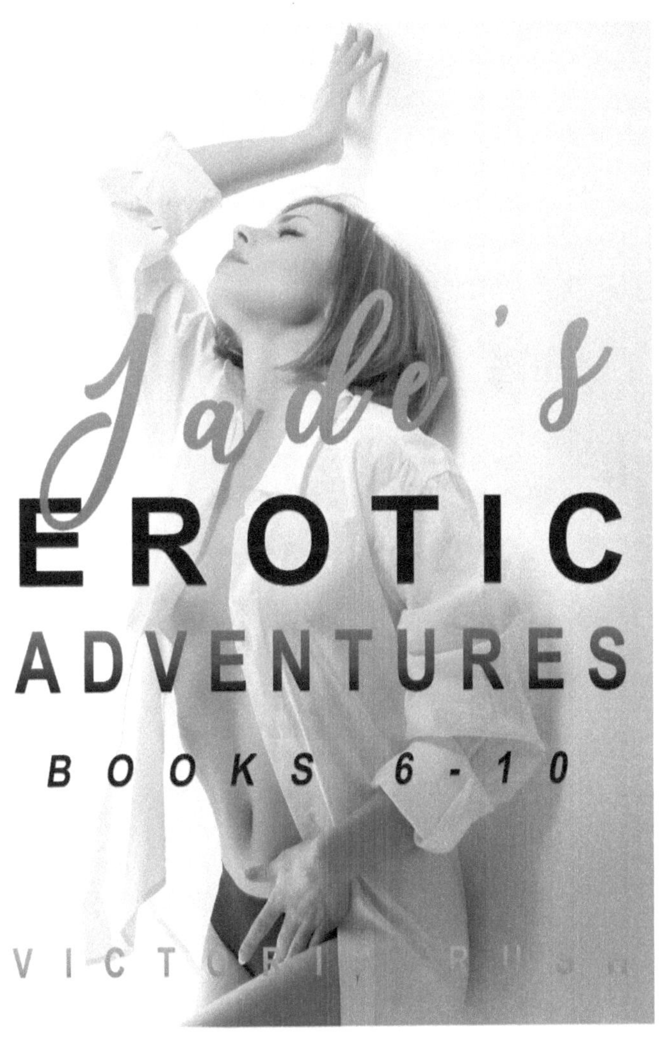

Books 6 - 10 in the bestselling series - now 60% off.

THE DOMINATRIX - PREVIEW

BONDAGE

On Saturday morning, I drove to Mistress Velvet's studio with a mix of trepidation and excitement. I was intrigued about being with a more dominant sexual partner, but I definitely felt uneasy about the idea of being tied up. As long as I remained in her clutches, I'd be completely at the mercy of someone who professed to enjoy inflicting pain.

As I drove across town, I kept shaking my head, unsure if I wanted to go through with it. I told myself that I'd check out her operation and that if I wasn't feeling entirely comfortable, I'd walk away. We'd have a long conversation about ground rules, and even if it ate into a portion of my paid session time, I needed to be sure I'd have final control over what happened to my body.

But something told me that this dominatrix was far more interested using me for her *own* pleasure than in watching someone else suffer. Anybody who was that concerned about protecting her safety with written contracts and session recordings must have long ago learned where to draw the line. The closer I got to her address, the tighter my thighs squeezed together, pinching my buzzing clit.

When my car's navigation system indicated that I'd arrived at my final designation, I looked around trying to locate Mistress Velvet's storefront. The street address comprised a long strip mall and there was no visible signage revealing her service location. I drove into the half-empty parking lot and stopped my car in front of the indicated unit number. A large plate-glass window covered the storefront with closed horizontal blinds.

Something didn't feel right. Everything was just too quiet and secluded. It would be the perfect location to torture and hold someone captive while you had your way with them. I was just about to turn around and drive away when I saw a young mother and child enter another shop a couple of doors down. I looked up and read the adjacent signs. There was a health clinic and a pet store on either side of the unmarked address. As a steady stream of patrons began to file in and out of the stores, my heart rate slowly returned to normal.

I got out of my car and walked up to the unmarked door to Unit Fourteen. Peering through the glass, I saw the familiar logo of Mistress Velvet dressed up in a naughty bodice riding a unicorn. Near the bottom of the sign was an arrow pointing down a long flight of stairs.

Of course she wouldn't broadcast her services for just any random passerby, I thought. *Who knows what kind of weirdos this kind of operation would attract? This is exactly the kind of service that should be by appointment only.*

I pulled on the handle and found it locked. I squinted at the side of the door and saw a small buzzer with a hand-written note reading *Press for Attendant.* I pressed the button and after a few seconds a female voice responded.

"Hello?" the voice said.

"My name is Jade," I replied. "I have a ten a.m. appointment with Mistress Velvet."

The door clicked and made a loud buzzing sound, and I pulled it open and scampered inside. The place had a strange musky scent, like a gym with slight undertones of lavender. The long flight of stairs led down to a closed door with a larger sign displaying Mistress Velvet's emblem. I walked down the steps and hesitated in front of the heavy door. There was a small peephole at eye height and I rapped on the surface with my knuckles.

A shadow flickered behind the peephole, then the door swung open. The beautiful redhead from Mistress Velvet's website smiled at me wearing a shiny vinyl trench coat with black fishnet stockings and high heels. Her huge breasts thrust against the reflective coating as her long curly locks cascaded over her shoulders. She was even more beautiful in the flesh, with high cheekbones, full pouty lips, and dark penetrating eyes.

"Welcome, Jade," she said, motioning me into the room. "I've been expecting you. Step into my dungeon."

When I entered the room, my eyes opened as wide as saucers. An assortment of whips and chains hung across the exposed brick walls. In each of the four corners rested a strange padded contraption. One could have passed for a conventional massage table, except for the wrist and leg cuffs strapped to either end. In the next corner stood a long padded board balancing on some kind of see-saw apparatus, with long leather straps running across the width of the board in one foot intervals. In the opposite corner rested a tall wooden throne-type chair with metal arm and foot restraints. In the final corner lay some kind of leather harness with a jumble of hopes and chains. Near the middle of the room, a long lever extended up from the floor, directly under a series of hooks and pulleys hanging down from the ceiling. If it weren't for a lone table holding an assortment of dildos and sex toys, I would have thought I was in some kind of medieval torture chamber.

"I see why you call this a *dungeon*," I said, nodding my head slowly. "It looks like more of a torture chamber."

"Everybody's a little taken back the first time they see my sex palace," the redhead nodded. "It looks scarier than it really is. I assure you, everything in this boudoir is designed to take you to new heights of pleasure."

"Only mine?" I said, noticing a huge strap-on dildo resting on the sex toy table.

"That depends on the client," she said, running her eyes up and down my body. "Under the right circumstances, we *both* can have a little fun."

I peered around the room at the assortment of bondage paraphernalia and narrowed my eyes.

"This is my first time doing something like this," I said. "Do you mind if we take a few minutes to discuss exactly what will be involved before we begin?"

"Of course," Velvet nodded. "I'd have it no other way. There are a few necessary preliminaries. Just keep in mind that I have another appointment at eleven. So we'll want to dispense with the formalities as quickly as possible in order to give you the maximum attention you deserve."

"Is there somewhere we can sit down?" I said. "I mean other than the torture rack or the throne chair?"

"Absolutely," Velvet chuckled, motioning in the direction of the sex toy table. "There are some comfortable chairs in this corner."

Velvet opened a collapsible chair and waited for me to sit down before sitting kitty-corner across the table. When she lifted her leg to cross her knees, I caught a fleeting glimpse of a black garter between her legs.

"What concerns do you have that I can assuage?"

"Well, mostly," I began tentatively, "I'm concerned about being tied up and having no ability to—*defend myself*. Will I be able to stop the proceedings at any time if I begin to feel uncomfortable?"

"Of course," she said, batting her long dark eyelashes. "We live in a civilized culture, after all. You'll always have the final say. I'm here to make you feel stimulated and excited, not to inflict unmitigated pain."

"So all I have to do is say 'stop' or 'no' when I want it to stop?"

"Technically, yes. Though I prefer each client to have a more elegant code word to terminate the proceedings. Just keep in mind that if you choose to deny me for any reason, that will automatically end the session and you won't be eligible for any refund of unused time. What would you like your code word to be?"

I paused to think of something less harsh than simply 'stop'.

"How about arrêtez? It means the same thing in French."

"That'll work," Velvet nodded. "But try to use it sparingly, since you can only say it once. I think you may find that the less control you have and the more uncomfortable you feel, the more invigorating the session will be. The whole point of BDSM is in giving complete control to your domme and in embracing the slave role."

My pussy pulsed at the mention of the word slave. I kept staring at the giant strap-on dildo on the other end of our table, thinking what Velvet had in mind for me.

"I understand," I nodded. "Where do we begin?"

Velvet reached into a drawer and passed a piece of paper and a pen across the table.

"I'll just need you to sign this waiver. And your credit card to process the rest of your payment."

"Of course," I said, reaching into my purse and passing her my card.

As Velvet processed my payment, I quickly scanned the contract. It was mostly standard boilerplate, limiting liability in the event of a dispute over the nature of services rendered. I was happy to see the clause referencing the recording of the proceedings and that I would be given the only tape upon successful completion of the session. The contract reiterated that Mistress Velvet would have complete and total authority to do whatever she pleased with me, so long as I didn't utter the agreed upon code word.

"Does everything appear satisfactory?" Velvet said, handing me the credit card voucher to sign.

"Yes, I think so," I said. "Although I'm a little confused by what 'satisfactory completion' of the session means."

"That's more for my protection than yours. It simply means that as long as I'm not physically threatened or harmed, you'll be given possession of the recording upon completion of the session. Not that I'm worried about you. But some of my male clients like to play pretty rough." Velvet pointed to a dark glass window on the far wall of the room. "Until then, everything will be securely filmed behind that wall."

I looked at the dark window and chuckled nervously.

"How do I know there isn't also some weirdo peeping at us behind that wall?"

"Fair question," Velvet said, beckoning me toward the door. "I like to be completely transparent at all times."

She punched in a code on the keypad lock, then swung

the door open for me to look inside. I peered into the closet-sized room and saw an old VHS video camera on a tripod, pointed toward the window.

"I like your style, Miss Velvet," I said, appreciating her abundance of caution.

"Shall we begin then?"

"Yes, I feel comfortable now."

Velvet stepped into the video room and pressed a button on the side of the camera and a red light begin to flash. Then she pulled the door closed and we returned to the sex toy table, where I signed the contract.

"Right then," she said, suddenly changing her tone. "From this point forward, you are to address me only as Mistress Velvet or Master. I will refer to you simply as Slave. Repeat the code word that you wish to use to cease all proceedings one last time. In the absence of this code word, you are to obey all of my commands. Is that understood?"

"Yes—Master," I smiled. "The code word is arrêtez."

"Good," Velvet said. "Now strip off all your clothes."

"Everything?"

"Everything."

I unbuttoned my blouse and slowly pulled it off my shoulders.

"Where shall I put them?" I said, looking at Velvet demurely.

"Hand them to me. I'll place them in a safe location."

I handed Velvet my blouse then unclasped my bra and passed it to her. Although she maintained a steely expression as she peered back and forth across my naked breasts, the quickening pace of her breathing as evidenced by her heaving breasts above her corset, betrayed her excitement.

"Now your pants," she ordered, glancing below my waist.

I unzipped my jeans and lowered them slowly to the

floor. Then I pulled off my sneakers and handed them to her. Finally, I pulled down my panties and held them out with an outstretched arm.

"What about you?" I said, running my eyes over her curvaceous figure hidden under her trench coat.

"I'm the one giving orders here, slave," she barked. "Now stand still while I appraise your figure."

She ran her eyes up and down my body, pausing for a long moment to stare at my bald hips and mound, then again at my nipples, which seemed to get harder and more erect the longer she stared at them.

"Not too shabby," she said, narrowing her eyes. "Now turn around."

I turned one-hundred-and-eighty degrees and stared at the dark window, smiling for the video camera.

"Spread your legs shoulder width apart and bend over ninety degrees."

As I followed Velvet's command, I felt the moisture beginning to accumulate on the inside of my labia.

"Very nice," she said. "Now turn around and face me again, with your legs spread shoulder width apart."

I turned around, and Velvet lowered her head to gaze at the bare folds of skin outlining my pussy.

"You'll do fine," she said. "I'm going to have a lovely time using and abusing your girlish figure. Wait here while I retrieve your harness."

Velvet hung up my clothes on a hook next to some whips and chains, then she disappeared behind me where I heard some rustling of clothes and equipment. When she returned to face me, she'd taken off her trench coat and was carrying a tangled assortment of leather, ropes, and chains. She kneeled down on the floor and spread out the equipment into a star shape, with the ropes angling out in four directions from a perforated leather harness.

When she stood back up, I ran my eyes wildly over her body. Her D-cup breasts spilled over the top of a black leather half-corset, with her large brown nipples pointing sensuously toward me above the seam. Her waist tapered to a narrow midsection, before flaring to wide, curvy hips, framed by a crotchless black leather garter supporting fishnet stockings with long thin black straps running up the front of her bare thighs. Her pussy, like mine, was entirely bare, revealing a large nub between her legs. I sagged at my knees, gasping at her gorgeous body.

"Lie down on the harness," Velvet commanded, directing her eyes to the floor.

"Can I just—" I pleaded, wanting a few more seconds to take in her magnificent figure.

"Lie down!" she commanded.

"Yes, Master," I demurred, kneeling down on the floor. "How do you want me—"

"Place your ass at the bottom of the harness, then lie back with your head toward the ropes. I'll take care of the rest."

I did as I was told, lying back against the cold perforated leather. The harness looked like a small hammock with large holes to permit maximum access to the recliner's skin. Velvet kneeled down and straddled my waist, and my pussy throbbed as I envisioned her rubbing herself against me. But instead she reached over my head and grabbed the ropes splayed out on the floor and began wrapping them tightly around my tits. She encircled each breast with the nylon cord, then ran a figure eight across the front of my chest and tied the two ends securely around the back of my neck.

My eyes widened at the thought of having a rope tied around my neck, but I began to relax when I realized the pressure point was behind my shoulders rather than over my throat. I peered down at my tightly bound boobs, noticing how they'd already swelled from the constricted circulation. My areolas had turned a dark shade of purple and my nipples stood out almost a full inch, tingling in arousal.

Velvet paused for a moment to appraise her handiwork then peered into my eyes with a sexy grin.

"Do you like that, my sexy little slave?" she purred. She grabbed my tits with her two hands and squeezed them roughly. "Because your nipples are definitely saying yes."

"Yes," I squeaked, arching my hips to press against her body.

Velvet spread her knees wider apart, placing her full weight on my abdomen, thumping my body back onto the floor. Then she lowered her head and sucked hard on each of my erect nipples for a few seconds, making a loud popping sound each time she removed her mouth. Her wet pussy writhed against my bare stomach as she pinned her body over mine.

"Fuck yes!" I exclaimed, letting her know in no uncertain terms that I was enjoying her attention.

Then she shimmied her hips over my hard mound and hipbones, spreading her juices over my midsection like she was marking me.

"I'm going to have a lot of fun with you before we're finished," she said. "But first I need to get you properly restrained so I can have my way with you."

She waddled up my body until her pussy rested just above my face, then she grabbed my arms and tied the ropes at the top of the harness tightly around my wrists. Then she threaded the loose ends through two eyelets and tied secure knots to hold my arms high above my head. When she finished binding my hands to the harness, she peered down to see me staring at her glistening labia. I extended my tongue trying to touch her throbbing clit, but she kneeled just far enough away for me not to reach her.

"You want to lick my pussy, slave?" she taunted. "You'll have to beg for it. But don't worry, there will be plenty of opportunities for you to satisfy me soon enough. Let's get those pretty little legs of yours pulled up with your arms. I want to have unfettered access to your sweet, moist kitty."

Velvet lifted her knee and turned around so she was straddling me in the other direction. She leaned forward, revealing her pink rosebud and dripping labia. When I lifted my head trying to reach her, she shifted her body in the other direction, toward my hips. She paused for a moment over my bound breasts and rubbed her pussy over each of my distended nipples until both of my tits were thoroughly coated with her sex juices. There was something incredibly sexy about her spreading her wetness all over my prostrated body while I could only stand there and watch. My hips twisted and convulsed, trying vainly to produce some friction against my aching clit.

When she reached my midsection, she straddled my hips again and titled forward at the waist, giving me another premium view of her tight rosebud and wide-open lips. Then she grabbed my legs and wound the other two ends of the loose ropes around my ankles while spreading my legs apart. When she finished, she stood up and pulled the ropes as far as she could toward my head, binding my ankles to my hands. I was now stretched as far into an accordion position as my body allowed, with my legs splayed and pulled behind my head. I looked between my legs and saw that my pussy was wide open, with my labia spread apart and my juices dripping down the crack of my ass.

"Now we're talking," Velvet smiled, standing over me, nodding approvingly. "It looks like you're already getting excited about the idea of being hog-tied for my amusement. But you haven't seen anything yet."

She stood over me for a moment, straddling my waist in her six-inch stilettos, then stepped slowly up toward my head. I peered nervously out of the corner of my eyes, fearing she might pinch my skin with her sharp heels, but she simply sneered as she got closer and closer to my breasts. When she reached my armpits, she spread her legs on either side of my shoulders and paused to let me peer up her long and magnificent body. Her legs seemed to go on forever, and above the sensuous cleft between her legs, her tits jutted out like ripe melons from the dark stem of her corset.

Her pussy was glistening in obvious excitement, and as I watched her juices begin to run down the inside of her thighs, I hoped they might eventually reach the sides of my body. But just as I envisioned she might let me have a small taste of her body, she stepped over my head and grabbed the top of my harness and fastened three chains with hooks to the top and two sides of my harness. Then she lifted the three ends of the chains toward a large metal hook hanging from the ceiling.

"What the—?" I muttered, realizing she intended to lift me up onto the hook.

"That's right," Velvet sneered. "I'm going to hang you from the rafters like a piece of meat. Then you'll really see who's in charge here."

She connected the ends of each chain to the large overhead hook, then she grabbed the lever poking up from the floor and began thrusting it forward and back. The slack in the chains tightened, and I began to feel myself lifting off the floor. Most of my weight was supported by the black leather harness, but I could definitely feel my arms and legs stretched tighter and wider with each pull of the lever. When my ass elevated to Velvet's hip level, she stopped cranking the lever and looked down at me. Every part of my body was pulled as high and far apart as possible. I peered down my midsection, seeing my tits squeezed into tight pyramids and my hips curled up toward my face, revealing the separated parts of my puffy lips spread into a wide and gleaming crevasse.

Velvet reached up onto the two chains supporting the sides of my harness and suddenly pulled them down, angling my body forty-five degrees forward.

"Do you like that, my sweet?" she said, looking deep into my eyes, stepping forward and rubbing her bare mound tantalizingly against my splayed pussy.

"Yes, Master," I said. "Please fuck me now. I want you to have your way with me."

"Oh I will, my slave. Don't you worry. When I'm finished with you, I'll have sprayed myself all over your tight little body and you'll have licked every square inch of me."

Velvet walked slowly around my suspended body until she was standing behind my head. Then she reached up and yanked down on the chain supporting the other end of my harness. I suddenly tilted forty-five degrees in the other direction, until my head dangled just under her dripping pussy. Then she turned around and planted her ass on my face.

"Lick my rosebud, slave," she commanded.

Read More

ABOUT THE AUTHOR

If you would like to receive notification of new books in Jade's Erotic Adventures, follow me at http://bookbub.com/authors/victoria-rush.

If you have a moment, please post a brief review on my Amazon book page at viewbook.at/pt . Even just a couple of sentences will help other readers find and enjoy this book as much as you hopefully did.

Follow, share, like, and comment at:

www.facebook.com/authorvictoriarush
www.pinterest.com/authorvictoriarush
www.twitter.com/authorvictoriarush
authorvictoriarush@outlook.com

Hope to see you again soon!